The Journey to Mermaid Kingdom

The Tail of the Mermaids Book 1

Celesta Thiessen
Keziah Thiessen
Priscilla Thiessen

CHAPTER 1

It was a sunny day in July. The Thiessen family was at the beach but they were all a little sad. They were going to have to move because they couldn't pay for their house anymore. Today would be the last time they would have a picnic at the ocean.

Mom and Dad were setting up the picnic. Ruth, the thirteen-year-old, and

Sammy, the five-year-old, were swimming. The seven-year-old-twins, Grace and Robbie, were collecting seashells. Their cats, Kitty and Blackie, were sniffing a pile of shells the children had found. Kitty was a brown tabby and Blackie was all black.

Suddenly, Grace spotted a small treasure chest in the sand! "Oh! I see a treasure chest! Let's go open it!" All four children rushed over and tried to open the treasure chest to see what was inside. They couldn't get it open.

"Mom, come help!" called Sammy. Mom came over and pulled on the lid, too.

The treasure chest popped open! A magical light shone out of it.

Suddenly, they all realized that they were now mermaids with wonderful looking tails! Their legs had turned into tails! The light touched the cats, too. They turned into mercats!

A voice came out of the light. "We give you the gift of the tail of the mermaids. We need your help. Follow the dolphins to Mermaid Kingdom! This treasure is yours to keep." The light faded.

Grace wiggled her beautiful tail. "Wow! This is amazing!"

"I wonder if we can breathe under water?" asked Ruth.

Mom looked at her tail. "Oh, no!"

Dad came rushing over. "What happened?"

Sammy crossed his arms. "We turned into mermaids. I don't want to be a mermaid."

"You're a merbrother," said Grace.

"We have…tails!" cried Mom.

"What are we going to do?" asked Dad.

"We're going to help the mermaids, of course," said Ruth.

"I think we *will* have to go and help the mermaids. Otherwise, how will we get our legs back?" said Mom.

Robbie looked into the treasure chest. "Look! Gold and gems!"

Dad looked into the treasure chest too. "This treasure is worth a lot of money. We will be able to use some of it to pay for our house and we will still have some left over."

"Yay! I never saw real treasure before! I'm so glad we get to keep it!" said Grace.

"I'm glad we won't have to move!" said Robbie. A car drove into the beach parking lot.

Dad closed the treasure chest, scooped it up and tucked it under his arm. "You should go now. I don't know what people would do if they saw mermaids."

"We will have to drag ourselves into the ocean," said Mom. "Everyone, drag yourself into the ocean."

Dad picked up Sammy and carried him into the ocean, because he was the youngest. Soon Mom and the other three children had dragged themselves into the ocean.

"What about the cats?" asked Sammy. The cats had dragged themselves to the edge of the water, following the children, but they weren't going in. They were lying on the shore, meowing sadly. Then, slowly, the cats pulled themselves into the water, meowing as they went.

"I don't think the cats like the water," said Robbie.

Mom ducked underwater. A moment later, she came up laughing. "Ruth! We *can* breathe underwater!" All the children tried it.

Robbie opened his eyes underwater. Kitty's face was right close to his face. He snorted in surprise and then started laughing.

"What's so funny?" asked Sammy.

"The cats have gotten used to it. They're swimming underwater too!" said Robbie.

Mom and the kids came to the surface again to say goodbye to Dad.

Dad waded into the water. He hugged Mom and then each of the children. "I'm going miss you all so much."

"Don't worry. I'll take good care of them," said Mom.

"It's time for our merpack to head out to sea!" said Grace. The five of them, along with their cats, swam out into the deep ocean.

The cats turned around and started swimming back to shore. But a large shark had snuck up behind them. The children saw that the cats were in trouble. They swam towards the cats.

The shark snapped at Blackie but the mercat darted out of the way. Then the shark lunged towards Kitty but she moved just in time!

"Mom!" Grace called. "We need to rescue the cats!" The children got between the cats and the shark.

"Go away," shouted Robbie.

"Bad shark! Bad shark!" shouted Sammy.

The shark circled around the children and the cats, waiting for its chance. Ruth swam down to the ocean floor and grabbed a rock. She swam back to her brothers and sister. She threw the rock at the shark. The rock hit the shark right on the nose. While the shark was distracted, Mom swam behind it and grabbed its tail so that it couldn't attack. But the shark was very strong. "I can't hold it much longer! Help! Someone help!"

A pod of dolphins heard Mom's cries and came straight away to help. When the shark saw the dolphins, it tried to swim in the other direction. So Mom let it go and the shark swam away.

"Thank you, dolphins!" said Mom. "You saved us!"

"You're welcome," said the dolphins. There were three dolphins - two adults and a little one. "We've come to lead you to the Mermaid Kingdom."

"Whoa! Dolphins!" said Sammy.

"This is Swimmy," said the mother dolphin, introducing the little one. "And my name is Luna because I love jumping for the moon! Luna means moon."

The father dolphin pushed his way forward. "My name is Current."

Suddenly, a blue tornado of light appeared, swirling in the water.

"Ahh!!!" cried Grace.

Sammy and Swimmy were sucked into the portal.

"Oh, no!" cried Mom.

"We have to go after them!" Ruth darted into the portal after Sammy.

Mom grabbed Robbie and Grace's hands and swam through the portal. The mercats followed them. The portal slammed closed right behind them, leaving Luna and Current trapped on the other side.

Instantly, they all arrived safely in a different and strange part of the ocean. It was dark, and seaweed was everywhere. When Swimmy saw that his parents weren't there, he started crying.

CHAPTER 2

"Oh no! Swimmy's parents!" cried Grace.

Mom put her arm around the little dolphin. "Don't worry, Swimmy. I'll take care of you until we find your parents." Swimmy snuggled into Mom and stopped crying.

Suddenly, a huge orange octopus swooshed up from the sea floor. "Ha, ha, ha! I'm the evil scientist octopus and you have fallen into my trap!"

The girls screamed in fright. The octopus was big enough to eat them all. He grabbed the mermaids, the mercats and Swimmy in his tentacles and dragged them back to his lab lair. Grace screamed the whole way. The boys wiggled to get free. Mom pushed against the tentacle as hard as she could. But they couldn't get away. The octopus threw them into a cage and slammed the door closed.

"What do you want with us?" cried Ruth.

"I will discover the secret of the tail of the mermaids. Because, one day, I will have legs and go to your world and become the greatest scientist that ever lived. Then everyone will bow down to my greatness! Ha! Ha! Ha!" He laughed an evil laugh.

"No! You can't do that!" shouted Ruth.

Lights came on in the cage and started scanning them. "Soon I will have the secret of the tail of the mermaids!" The evil scientist octopus swam out of the room.

"What are we going to do?" asked Robbie.

"I see the key hanging on the wall over there." Mom reached her arm through the bars but she couldn't reach the key. Swimmy started crying again. It's very sad to see a dolphin cry.

"It's going to be okay, Swimmy," said Sammy.

"Yeah," said Robbie. "We'll think of something."

"Oh, no!" cried Mom. "Swimmy needs air to breathe! But he's trapped in the cage!"

Swimmy sniffed loudly and cuddled into mom. "The mermaids gave us magic. We can breathe water now. But I'm scared."

Two smaller octopuses swam into the room. One of them was green and red and the other one was red and purple. "What did Uncle Naturae do now?" asked the red and purple one.

"Who are you?" asked Sammy.

"I'm Iaculari," said the red and green octopus.

"I'm Perdere," said the red and purple octopus. "We're Professor Naturae's nephews."

"Can you help us?" asked Mom.

"Sure," replied Iaculari. "We would be glad to help you!"

"Thank you! Can you pass me the key that's hanging on the wall?" asked Mom.

"No, we have to make it look like you got out yourselves. That way, we won't get in trouble," said Perdere.

"Handing them the key would be so easy," said Iaculari.

"Handing them the key is not the solution," said Perdere. "Come with me. I have a plan." The two octopuses left the room.

"Do you think they're really going to help us?" asked Robbie.

"I sure hope so," said Mom.

***

Perdere and Iaculari swam farther into their uncle's lab.

"We are going to operate uncle's portal to get the adult dolphins here. Then the adult dolphins will rescue them," said Perdere.

"I like that plan," said Iaculari.

Perdere swam over to the portal-maker machine. "I hope we don't need a key to turn this on."

"I think you press this button here," said Iaculari.

"Are you sure?" asked Perdere. "There are so many buttons."

"I think so. That's what I remember."

"Okay then." Perdere pressed the button. The machine hummed to life.

"What do we do now?" asked Iaculari.

"I think it responds to voice commands. Let me try," said Perdere. "Bring Current and Luna here."

"Wait! How did you know their names?" asked Iaculari.

"I know their names because I looked at Uncle Naturae's clipboard. He has all his evil plans written down there," Perdere said.

A big, blue, swirling portal flashed open and sucked the adult dolphins in.

"Where are they now?" asked Iaculari.

"They must have landed in the same place that the mermaids did."

They swam out into the ocean to find the adult dolphins. When they found them, Luna and Current looked mad.

"We know where Swimmy is," said Perdere.

Current swam at the young octopuses. "You had better tell us right now!"

"They're in there!" Perdere cried, pointing towards the lab lair.

"Come on. We'll show you," said Iaculari. "We're helping because we don't like our uncle's evil plans." They all swam towards the lab lair, with Iaculari leading the way.

"They are right in there and the key to the cage is hanging on the wall," said Perdere.

"Now, we've got to get out of here so Uncle Naturae doesn't find out that we've helped them!" said Iaculari. The young octopuses swam away as fast as they could.

Luna and Current went into the lab lair. They found the mermaids, the mercats and Swimmy in a cage. Swimmy squealed in delight to see his parents.

"Shh," said Luna, "we have come to get you out."

Mom pointed to the wall. "The keys are hanging right there."

Current grabbed the keys in his mouth. An alarm started ringing. The big octopus swam into the lab lair. The two smaller octopuses, Iaculari and Perdere, swam in behind him.

"Oh, no!" cried Sammy.

"What?!" The evil scientist octopus pointed at Swimmy's parents. "How did they get here?"

Blackie, who had been watching the octopus tentacles swish back and forth, suddenly pounced out through the space between the bars and attacked, biting one tentacle with all his might.

"Ouch!" Scientist Naturae whipped around to see who had bitten him. Blackie darted back into the cage.

"Quick, Current," said Mom, "pass me the keys!"

Current swam towards the cage but he wasn't fast enough. Scientist Naturae caught Current in one of his tentacles. "Well, isn't this a happy reunion. Now you're all back together." Scientist Naturae caught Luna too, and then he ripped the keys away from Current. He opened the cage and threw the adult dolphins in with everyone else.

Quickly, Ruth darted out the open door and grabbed the keys. Robbie and Sammy tried to get out too but Scientist

Naturae shoved them back in. While he was distracted, Ruth turned the lights off.

"Eeek!!! Let me out of here!" Scientist Naturae swam out of the room. Everyone got out of the cage.

"That was easy," said Ruth.

"I think our uncle is afraid of the dark," said Iaculari.

"Go quickly before he comes back!" said Perdere.

CHAPTER 3

Everyone was happy to be out of the cage and back together again. They knew they had to continue their journey to Mermaid Kingdom.

"Where are we?" asked Mom. "How do we get to the Mermaid Kingdom from here?"

"I know this place," said Current. "I know the way."

"How far did we go in the portal? Are we closer now or farther?" asked Ruth.

Luna sighed. "We're farther." The mermaids quickly swam out of the lab lair with the dolphins.

"Good-bye and good luck," said Iaculari.

"Stay away from portals," said Perdere. The young octopuses swam off to find their crazy uncle.

Current led the way, swimming through the ocean.

"How far is it to Mermaid Kingdom?" asked Grace.

"It would take twenty-eight hours if we swam it all at once. But we'll have to stop to sleep sometime," said Current.

As they swam, they saw more and more seaweed. "We are entering the Kelp forest," said Luna.

"It's important that we all stick together," said Current.

"Let's hold hands," said Mom. The mermaids all took each other's hands.

"But what about our mercats?" said Sammy.

"We could tie them to ourselves with a kelp leash," suggested Ruth.

Mom let go of the children's hands. "Good idea. Ruth, help me make two leashes."

Mom and Ruth pulled two long kelp strands free from the kelp forest. Mom made a little harness for Kitty and tied the other end to her own waist. Ruth copied her and tied Blackie to herself.

"Okay, now we are ready," said Ruth. When the mermaids looked up, they realized that the dolphins were nowhere in sight.

"Oh, no!" said Grace.

"They must not have realized that we stopped," said Ruth.

"We'll have to wait here for them. I don't think we should venture into the kelp forest alone," said Mom.

Suddenly, a large shadow passed quickly overhead. They looked up and screamed. Above them was a giant sea serpent! It was green, with huge red eyes. Its mouth and long, sharp teeth were green with slime. Its long, sharp claws flexed as it looked down at them. The sea serpent dove towards them. Ruth grabbed a piece of coral and got ready. When the sea serpent got close, she whacked it on the head.

The sea serpent grabbed Ruth in its claw and swam away.

"Oh, no!" cried Sammy.

"We need to go after her!" said Grace.

"But the dolphins won't know where we went," said Robbie.

"We'll have to split up," said Grace.

"Splitting up is never a good idea," said Mom. "The dolphins will find us. We need to go save Ruth."

"I hope Ruth doesn't get eaten!" said Sammy. The mermaids swam after the sea serpent. They couldn't catch up but they were able to keep him in sight so that they could follow him.

***

Meanwhile, the serpent clutched Ruth in his sharp claws. Ruth looked in disgust at the slime dripping out of his mouth.

"You'd better not get that on me!" she yelled as she pushed and tried to get away. The serpent closed his claws a little tighter. Ruth yelped.

The serpent slowed down. Ruth looked around. She had been here before. It had taken her back to the lab lair! The serpent let Ruth go. She tried to swim away but was caught by an orange tentacle.

It was the evil scientist octopus! "You thought it was that easy? I don't think so! I've got you now! Ha, ha, ha!" He laughed his evil laugh. "You didn't expect my mutant sea serpent to come after you, did you? Ha, ha, ha!" He took Ruth back into his lab lair and threw her into the cage. "Perfect! Now I just need to wait for your family to come for you. Then you will all be my prisoners again and I will find the secret of the tail of the mermaids. Ha, ha, ha!" He slammed the cage door closed. This time, he took the keys away with him.

Ruth untied Blackie, who darted out between the bars and swam out of the lab lair. If only that cat could help her somehow.

***

Ruth's family had followed the sea serpent all the way back to the lab lair. When they got there, Blackie swam over to the rest of the family.

"Oh, no!" said Sammy. "That bad octopus has Ruth!"

"I wish that his life would be over!" said Grace.

"I agree!" said Robbie.

"Don't say that, Kids," said Mom. "Maybe he will have a change of heart and become a good octopus one day."

"But, *today*, he has our sister trapped in a cage!" said Robbie.

"What do we do?" asked Sammy.

Mom called the children over to a big rock. "I'm going to go in for Ruth. You all hide here. And keep the cats with you."

"But, Mom, what if you get caught too?!" said Robbie.

"Then you three will still be free to try to save us."

"But I thought splitting up is never a good idea," said Grace.

"It is when I'm keeping you safe," said Mom. She swam away into the lab lair. There, she found Ruth in the cage.

"Mom!" said Ruth.

"Where's the key?" Mom whispered.

"The evil octopus has it."

Just then, the evil scientist octopus swam into the room. He grabbed Ruth's mom, unlocked and opened the cage door, and threw her in. This time, he was careful not to let Ruth swim out.

"Ha, ha! I've got you now, and I will get the mermaid's secret!"

CHAPTER 4

Meanwhile, outside, the kids saw the friendly octopuses.

Robbie called to them. "We're over here." The octopuses swam over to the kids. Robbie told them about Ruth and their mother.

"What are we going to do?" asked Sammy.

"We can go check to see what Uncle Naturae is doing," said Iaculari. The young octopuses swam into the lab lair. The mercats followed them.

What nobody knew was that the mermaid's magic had made the cats smarter. It had happened slowly so that even the cats didn't know it at first. The family didn't know it either. But, now, the cats could understand what the children and the octopuses were saying. They realized that they could talk too, if they wanted to.

They found both Ruth and her mother in the cage. Scientist Naturae wasn't in the room.

"I'm sorry Uncle Naturae captured you again," said Iaculari.

"Do you know where your uncle put the key?" asked Mom.

"No, we don't know where he put it," said Iaculari.

Without saying a word, the mercats swam off to look for the key.

"Oh, no! The cats are wandering off again," said Ruth.

"We have bigger things to worry about," said Mom.

***

The mercats swam deeper into the creepy lab lair. There, they saw all sorts of horrible experiments: robotic-looking devices and glowing creatures in jars. There was also a large cage of sea dragons!

A blue sea dragon spoke. "Cats. Hey, Cats! Over here!"

The mercats looked at the cage full of dragons suspiciously. Just then, they heard the evil scientist octopus swimming towards them.

A red sea dragon said, "Come hide in here. If you hide behind us in the cage, the octopus won't see you."

"Is that a good idea?" asked Kitty.

Blackie darted into the cage. But Kitty swam in the other direction. The octopus swished passed and he didn't see the mercats. A dark grey dragon tried to take a chomp out of Blackie but a green dragon stopped him. Blackie darted back out of the cage.

"See, I was right," said Kitty. "You shouldn't have gone in there."

"I didn't die," said Blackie, "so I was right too."

"But you nearly did. That creature tried to eat you!"

"Nearly doesn't count," said Blackie.

"We're not creatures," said the blue dragon.

"Of course you are, silly creature," said Kitty.

The blue dragon said, "If we're creatures, you're creatures."

"We're cats," said Kitty, haughtily.

"Mercats, to be exact," said Blackie.

"And *we're* dragons," said the blue dragon.

The red dragon said, "I agree." You see, the red dragon was very agreeable and liked to get along with others.

"Can you let us out?" asked the green dragon.

"I don't think that's a good idea," said Kitty.

"We wouldn't eat you," said the dark grey dragon with a sly grin.

"Well, most of us wouldn't, anyway," said the blue dragon.

"I agree," said the red dragon again.

"If you let us out, we'll help you!" said the blue dragon.

"How do we know we can trust you?" asked Kitty.

"How do we let you out?" asked Blackie.

"The second question is easy," said the blue dragon. "To let us out, you just press the red button on the wall over there."

Blackie darted over to the wall and pressed the button with his paw.

"Blackie, what are you doing!?" cried Kitty.

There was a metal click as the lock on the cage released. The blue dragon shoved the door open and swam out. "Well, thank you, Blackie."

The dark grey dragon swam from the cage, with a roar and headed straight for Kitty.

The blue dragon pushed the dark grey one into the wall. "Do you want the scientist to hear us?" he demanded. "If you want your freedom, just swim away."

"Or we'll put you back into that cage!" added the green dragon.

"I agree," said the red dragon.

The dark grey dragon turned and swam away towards the exit of the lab lair.

Two other dragons swam out of the cage. They were both teal and they had red spikes on their tails. Flames sprang from the red spikes. One was a grown-up and one was a little baby. The adult teal dragon asked the cats, "Who are you?"

"I am Blackie."

"And I am Kitty. We are rescuing our owners."

"They are in a cage. Do you know where the key is?" asked Blackie.

"Naturae has it," said the Red dragon.

"How can we get the key?" asked Kitty.

"We won't need the key for the cage," said the blue dragon. "We can just smash that cage open. It wasn't designed to keep *us* out."

"I agree," said the red dragon.

The mercats and the dragons went back through the lab lair to the cage where Ruth and her mother were trapped. Ruth's mother screamed when she saw the dragons.

"Oh, don't worry about them. These dragons are friendly," said Blackie.

"Mostly. Probably," said Kitty.

"What?! The cats are talking now?" exclaimed Mom.

"Of course the cats are talking. Dolphins can talk. Dragons are real. It only makes sense!" said Ruth.

"Stand back!" said the green dragon. "One cage-smashing coming up!"

Ruth and Mom moved to the back of the cage. All the dragons started smashing the cage with their tales. The pounding broke the hinges and the door fell open. Ruth rushed out of the cage, with Mom right behind her.

"Let's get all the way away this time," said Mom.

"Yes, let's. I never want to see this horrible place again," said Kitty.

"But I'll miss the dragons," said Blackie.

"I like the dragons too," said Ruth.

"We can't stay here," said the green dragon.

"What are we to do? Bring us with you," said the blue dragon to the mermaids.

"I agree," said the red dragon.

So they all swam out of the lab lair together. They found Grace, Robbie and Sammy, right where Mom had left them.

"Time to go!" shouted Mom.

The evil scientist octopus came out of the lab lair just as they were making their getaway. But he stopped when he saw the dragons.

"Oh, no! What have you done? The dragons are uncontrollable!" cried Naturae.

CHAPTER 5

No one paid any attention to the octopus and they swam away as fast as they could. Pretty soon, they reached the kelp forest. There, they found the dolphins waiting for them.

"There you are!" cried Luna.

"We were so worried," said Swimmy.

"What are those creatures?" asked Current.

"For the second time today, we're not creatures. We're dragons!" said the blue dragon.

"Are they safe?" asked Luna.

"Probably. Mostly," said Kitty.

"Yay! The mercats are talking now!" Swimmy clapped his fins together.

Current patted Swimmy. "We must hurry to reach the Mermaid Kingdom. Our time is running out!" said Current.

"This way," said Luna. The dolphins turned to enter the kelp forest.

Suddenly, there was a boom in the distance. A shockwave ripped past them in the water, pushing them down to the sea floor.

"What was that?!" asked Robbie. They all looked in the direction the sound had come from. In the distance, the seaweed was on fire.

"Oh, no!" said Grace.

"How can there be fire under the water?" asked Mom.

"Sea dragon fire," said the green dragon.

"Well, now we know what direction the dark grey dragon went in," said the blue dragon.

The teal mamma dragon pulled her baby dragon close. "He's a very bad dragon," she whispered. The fire was getting larger.

"How do we put out a fire under water?" asked Ruth.

"Air or sand will put out a sea dragon's fire," said the mamma teal dragon. "And we *must* put it out or it will burn down the whole ocean."

"No way. We have to go back to the lab lair *again*?" asked Robbie.

"We have to go back," said the green dragon.

"I agree," said the red dragon.

Current nodded. "We'll have to go back to put the fire out. Otherwise, the whole ocean may be in danger." Reluctantly, they all turned back towards the lab lair.

When they got there, they found the scientist octopus and the two young octopuses frantically throwing sand on the fire that was near the lab lair.

"You came back," said Naturae.

"We need to work together to put this fire out," said Mom. "Do you have shovels we could use to help?"

Iaculari darted away. "I'll get shovels for you."

The dolphins and dragons swam up to the surface and gulped air to spray at the fire. Iaculari came back with five shovels so that the mermaids could help.

"I don't know if this is going to work," said Sammy.

"It has to work," said Mom. "We must save the ocean."

The cats scooped up sand with their tails and flung it at the fire. "I'm helping," said Blackie. Kitty glared at Blackie. She didn't like helping but she was anyway.

Soon, the good dragons and dolphins returned and sprayed air at the fire. With everyone working together, it didn't take long to put the fire out.

"Now, where is that dark grey dragon?" asked the blue dragon.

"He's much too dangerous to be out here," said the teal mamma dragon.

"I agree," said the red dragon.

The scientist octopus looked at everyone. "I need help getting the grey dragon back."

"I hope you're not planning to get us back too," said the blue dragon.

"I will grant the rest of you your freedom if you help me recapture the grey," said Naturae.

"But what about Mermaid Kingdom?" asked Mom. "They need us right away."

Naturae sighed. "I'll teleport you there after we recapture the grey."

"How do we know we can trust you?" asked Robbie.

"We don't. But if he betrays us, it will be all of us against one of him," said the blue dragon.

"Uncle Naturae will keep his promise," said Perdere. "Right, Uncle?"

Naturae sighed. "Of course."

"I have a plan," said Mom. "Naturae, bring a big cage out here."

The evil scientist octopus wasn't used to being ordered around. But he took one look at the dragons and he went to get a cage. "Boys, come help me carry it," he said to his nephews.

"Now, we all need to gather seaweed," said Mom.

"Why?" asked the blue dragon.

"You'll see. Just hurry," said Mom. The mermaids, dolphins and dragons started gathering the seaweed. Blackie tried to pull up a piece of seaweed but it was too hard for him.

Blackie gave up pulling the weed. "What can we do?"

"You cats will get to be the heroes," said Mom. "I'm glad you're so much smarter now."

Soon Scientist Naturae was back with the cage.

"Put the cage right there," Mom instructed. "Now, everyone put the seaweed all around so that you can't see that it's the cage." In a few minutes, the cage was hidden behind the seaweed.

"Now what?" asked Kitty.

"Now you cats start meowing while the rest of us get out of sight," said Mom.

"Wait a minute," said Blackie. "Are we bait?"

"Someone has to lure that dragon into the cage. And you are the only ones that can get out through the bars," said Mom. Everyone hid except for the mercats. "Start meowing," called Mom. Kitty meowed softly.

"You can do much better than that," called Sammy. "We hear how loud you meow every night at home."

The cats started meowing loudly. A roar sounded in the distance. The dark grey dragon had heard the cats. Fiercely, the dark grey dragon charged.

"I'll get you this time," said the dark grey dragon to the cats. He swam at the cats. They scooted into the cage. The dark grey dragon followed them in.

"It's working!" shouted Grace.

The blue dragon swam forward and slammed the cage shut. "You forgot to plan who should close the cage door. Luckily, *I* saved the day."

The mercats darted out of the cage. "We did it. We are heroes!" said Blackie.

The dark grey dragon roared. "Let me out of here! I'll get you for this! I'll get you all!!!"

"Well, if you hadn't tried to burn down the ocean, you wouldn't be in there," said the blue dragon to the grey.

The teal dragon looked over at the scientist octopus. "Now for that portal transport."

"Yes," said Current. "We're late. We must get to Mermaid Kingdom now."

The scientist octopus looked at the four big dragons staring at him. The blue dragon growled at him. Naturae looked at the mermaids and then at the dragons again. This time, all the dragons growled.

"Uh, right. Of course. Come this way to the portal machine." Naturae led the group into his lab lair. When they got to the machine, he turned it on. A swirling blue light appeared in the room. It flashed, sucking in all the dragons, dolphins, mermaids and mercats. Blue light swirled all around them. The portal spit them out. They opened their eyes to a most wondrous sight.

"Welcome to Mermaid Kingdom," said Luna.

KITTY CASTLE BOOKS

Get all the Kitty Castle books on Amazon!

KITTY CASTLE 1 - NIGHTCAT

KITTY CASTLE 2 - SURPRISES!

KITTY CASTLE 3 - ANSWERS!

KITTY CASTLE 4 - MYSTERY!

KITTY CASTLE 5 – REUNION

KITTY CASTLE 6 - CELEBRATIONS

If you liked this book, please leave us a great review on Amazon.com! Thanks for reading!

Made in the USA
Coppell, TX
21 December 2020